AF605591

TO :
FROM :
TODAY'S DATE :

First published in Australia by Affirm Press, 2023
Boon Wurrung Country
28 Thistlethwaite Street,
South Melbourne, VIC 3205
10 9 8 7 6 5 4 3 2 1

First published in the United Kingdom in 2023 by b small publishing ltd.
www.bsmall.co.uk

ISBN 9781922848239

Editorial by Sam Hutchinson.
Design and illustration by Vicky Barker.

Printed in China by WKT Co. Ltd.

My MUMMY and ME

A KEEPSAKE BOOK

WRITTEN BY
SAM HUTCHINSON

ILLUSTRATED BY
VICKY BARKER

This is my mummy!

STICK PHOTO
IN HERE!

Her first name is ....

She is .... years old

This is me!

STICK PHOTO
IN HERE!

My first name is ....

I am .... years old

My mummy's full name is

....

Her date of birth is

....

She was born in

....

She has .... siblings

Was your mummy born where you live now?
Look up her place of birth on a map
... even if it is only a few streets away!

My full name is

....

My date of birth is

....

I was born in

....

I have .... siblings

Do you know where your name comes from?
Who chose it? Does it have a special meaning?
Design a badge all about your name.

My mummy's height is

....

Her hair colour is

....

Her hair length is

....

Her eye colour is

....

Draw a picture of
your mummy!

My height is

....

My mummy is .... taller than me

My hair colour is

....

My hair length is

....

My eye colour is

....

Do you look similar to your mummy?
Do you have the same hair colour?
How about your mummy's mummy —
your grandparent! — do they look similar?

Draw a picture of yourself!
Make sure to sign your drawing,
like a famous artist.

The school my mummy went to is called

Her favourite subject was

Her least favourite subject was

Did your mummy do any activities at school or after school? Write about them here.

Ask your mummy if she has any photos or certificates you can see.

My school is called

My favourite subject is

My least favourite subject is

Do you do any activities at school or after school?
Are they similar to the activities your mummy did?
Write about a time that your mummy helped you
with something at school or after school.

When I am at school or learning at home, my mummy spends her time

....

....

....

Stick a photo or draw a picture here

Stick a photo or draw a picture here

When mummy was my age she dreamed of being a

....

....

....

When I am my mummy's age I want to be doing ...

My mummy's favourite colour is

....

My mummy's favourite piece of clothing is

....

Design a T-shirt that you think your mummy will love!

My favourite colour is

....

My favourite piece of clothing is

....

Draw a picture of you and your mummy wearing matching clothes.

Tell a funny story or draw a comic strip that will make your mummy laugh!

My mummy's favourite song is

....

The name of the band or the singer is

....

My mummy loves this song because

....

....

....

I think this song is

....

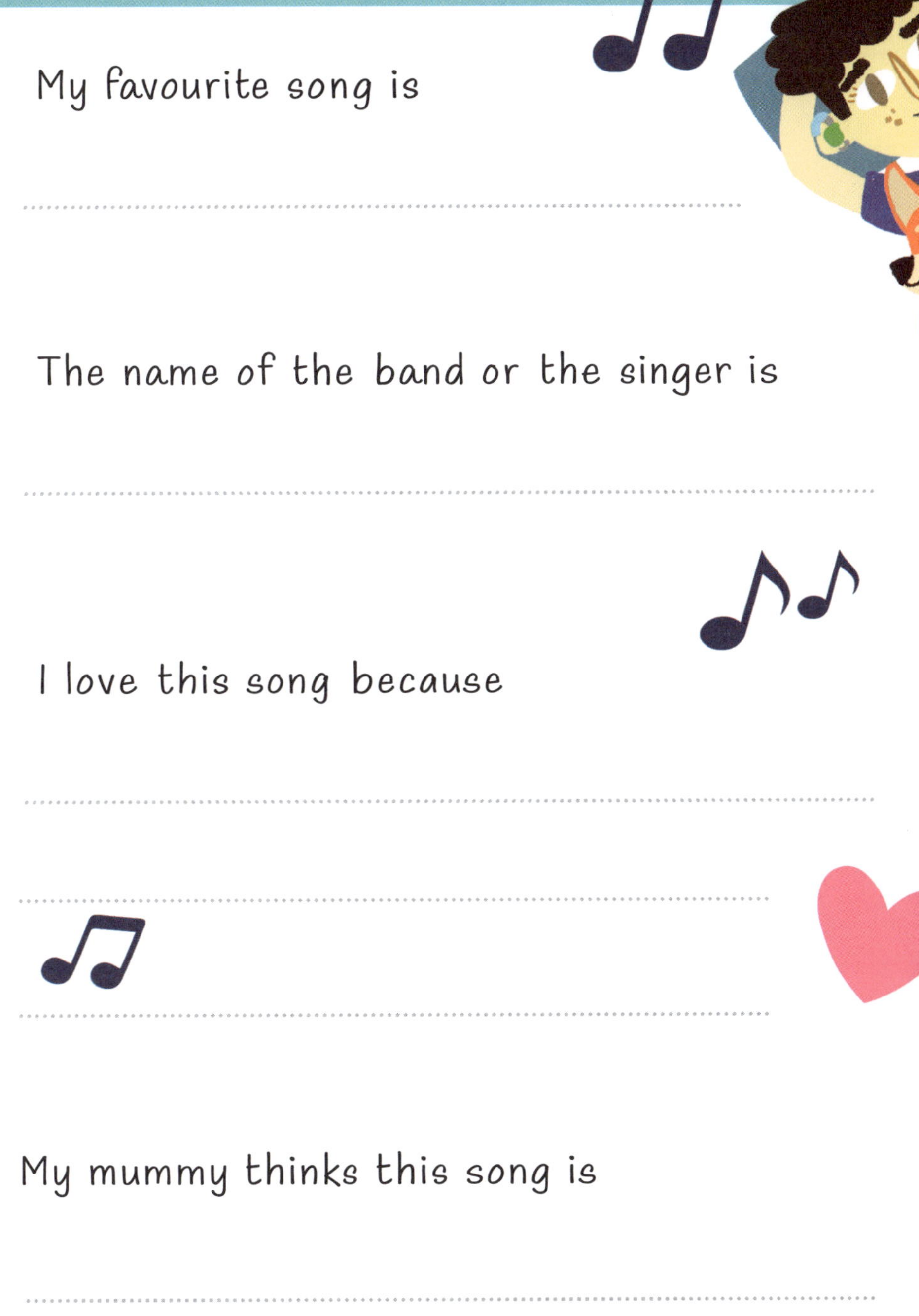

My favourite song is

....

The name of the band or the singer is

....

I love this song because

....

....

....

My mummy thinks this song is

....

For breakfast, my mummy likes to eat

....

For lunch, my mummy likes to eat

....

For dinner, my mummy likes to eat

....

Her favourite food is ....

Her least favourite food is ....

She can cook .... really well!

Draw a picture here

For breakfast, I like to eat

....

For lunch, I like to eat

....

For dinner, I like to eat

....

My favourite food is ....

My least favourite food is ....

I can cook .... really well!

Draw a picture here

Using three different colours, circle words that describe you in one colour, circle words that describe your mummy in another colour and, in a third colour, circle words that describe you both.

Kind

Funny

Silly

Serious

Outgoing

Fun

Tidy

Confident

Friendly

Private

Quiet

Energetic

Caring

Calm

Thoughtful

My perfect day with my mummy would involve:

In the morning, we

....

....

....

At lunchtime, we

....

....

....

In the afternoon, we

....

....

....

In the evening, we

Draw you and your mummy together at the end of a happy day together! You can stick in a photograph if you prefer.

My mummy travels around by

....

Draw a picture of your mummy and her favourite mode of transport!

When I am my mummy's age,
I will travel around in my

....

Draw a picture of your futuristic mode of transport!

My mummy's favourite hobbies include:

STICK PHOTO IN HERE!

My favourite hobbies include:

....

....

....

....

....

One thing we love to do together is:

....

One thing we would like to do together in the future is:

....

Finish writing this poem about your mummy!

I know my mummy loves me
She says it every day ...